Dedication:

To the keiki of Hawai'i,

Mālama i ke kai ~ Take care of the ocean

Acknowledgement:

Mahalo to marine biologist Ann Fielding for reviewing Iki's glossary and species identification list. Your dedication to education and conservation inspires me.

ISLAND HERITAGE™
PUBLISHING
A DIVISION OF THE MADDEN CORPORATION

94-411 Kō'aki Street
Waipahu, Hawai'i 96797-2806
Orders: (800) 468-2800
Information: (808) 564-8800
Fax: (808) 564-8877
welcometotheislands.com

ISBN: 0-89610-019-7
Second Edition, Second Printing—2017
COP 172808

iki
the littlest 'opihi

written & illustrated by Tammy Yee

ISLAND HERITAGE™
PUBLISHING

Once upon a time, a crowd of seashells lived on a rocky shore in Hawai'i.
Twice a day, the snails would creep along the ocean's edge, following the push
and pull of the tide.

Round *pipipi* and speckled *pūpū kōlea* dotted the surf-swept shore.

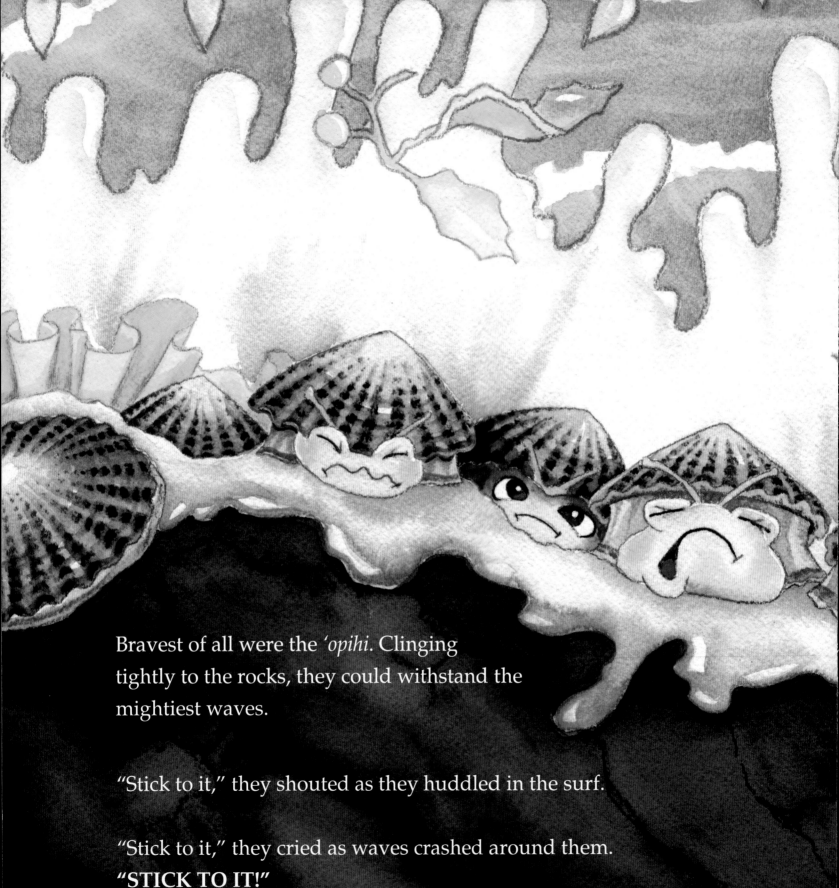

Bravest of all were the 'opihi. Clinging
tightly to the rocks, they could withstand the
mightiest waves.

"Stick to it," they shouted as they huddled in the surf.

"Stick to it," they cried as waves crashed around them.
"STICK TO IT!"

Iki was the littlest 'opihi of all. He was small and squat with a teeny-weeny shell that he carried like a shield on his back. Iki spent many days and nights as a larva, drifting merrily in the ocean. He floated far and wide, with not a worry in the world.

Soon it was time for Iki to find a rock and settle down.

"Settle down," said the other 'opihi as they found homes on the rocks.
"Settle down," cried the seashells from the shore.
"SETTLE DOWN!"

But Iki wouldn't settle down. He wanted to see the world.
He drifted away, far and wide.

In time, the ocean current carried Iki to the coral reef. Sea fans towered above him, swaying in the tide. Anemones bloomed like daisies in fields of sea lettuce. Schools of fish swam by.

"THE WORLD!" Iki shouted. Now he was ready to settle down with his friends on the rocky shore.

Above, a shark gnashed his teeth as he swam by.

But Iki wasn't worried. He was too tiny for a shark to see.
So onward he crawled, at a snail's pace.

Ahead, tentacles thrashed as a *he'e* wrestled a cowry into her den.

But Iki wasn't worried. He was too tiny for a *he'e* to eat. Still, he crawled a little faster toward the shore.

On a sandy ridge, a crab waved his claws. Two anemones, like palm trees, were planted on his back. But Iki wasn't worried. He was too tiny for a crab to notice. Wasn't he?

The crab grabbed Iki.

"Stick to it," Iki said as he hunkered beneath his shell.

"Stick to it," he grumbled as he dug his foot into the sand.
"STICK TO IT!"

But there was nothing for him to stick to.

"You're a funny-looking anemone," said the crab. He plucked Iki from the
sand and stuck him on his back.

Iki looked up. A big anemone on the right. A big anemone on the left. And little Iki in the middle, on the back of a lumbering crab. Iki spread his foot and held on for dear life.

The anemones smiled down at him.
"Look! A new neighbor! Let's hope he doesn't grow too big..."

"Or eat too much..."

"I'm looking for my friends on the rocky shore. Have you seen them?" asked Iki.

"No, but that's where we're going, too! So stick to it and enjoy the ride."

On the crab's back, no shark would bother him. No *he'e* would eat him. And crabs? He had a crab of his very own! And what a messy eater he was. Iki and the anemones had plenty to eat.

The anemones were very kind. They, too, had seen the world and had many fine stories to share. When they reached the rocky shore, Iki lifted his foot and tumbled off the crab's back.

"Goodbye," waved the anemones.

Iki found a spot among the other 'opihi and settled down beneath the pounding surf. Twice a day, he and his friends followed the ebb and flow of the tide.

Sometimes the other 'opihi whispered among themselves, "He's a wanderer. He'll never stick to it."

Iki ignored them.

One day, an *'opihi* picker visited Iki's rock. He used a sharp knife to pry the seashells from the rock. Then he placed them in a bag. The picker held tight as waves crashed around him.

The picker came to Iki and worked his knife under the *'opihi's* shell. Iki gripped the rock and held tight.

"Stick to it," Iki told himself.

A wave smashed into the picker, knocking
him from the rocks. He clung to his knife,
which was still stuck under Iki's shell.

24

"Stick to it," Iki shouted as the wave tried to pull the picker out to sea.

"STICK TO IT!"

The wave roared by. Iki let go of the rock and tumbled into the surf. The *'opihi* picker was safe. Together they were washed onto the sandy beach.

"This is it," thought Iki.

The picker held Iki in his hand. Iki's shell was chipped from the picker's knife.

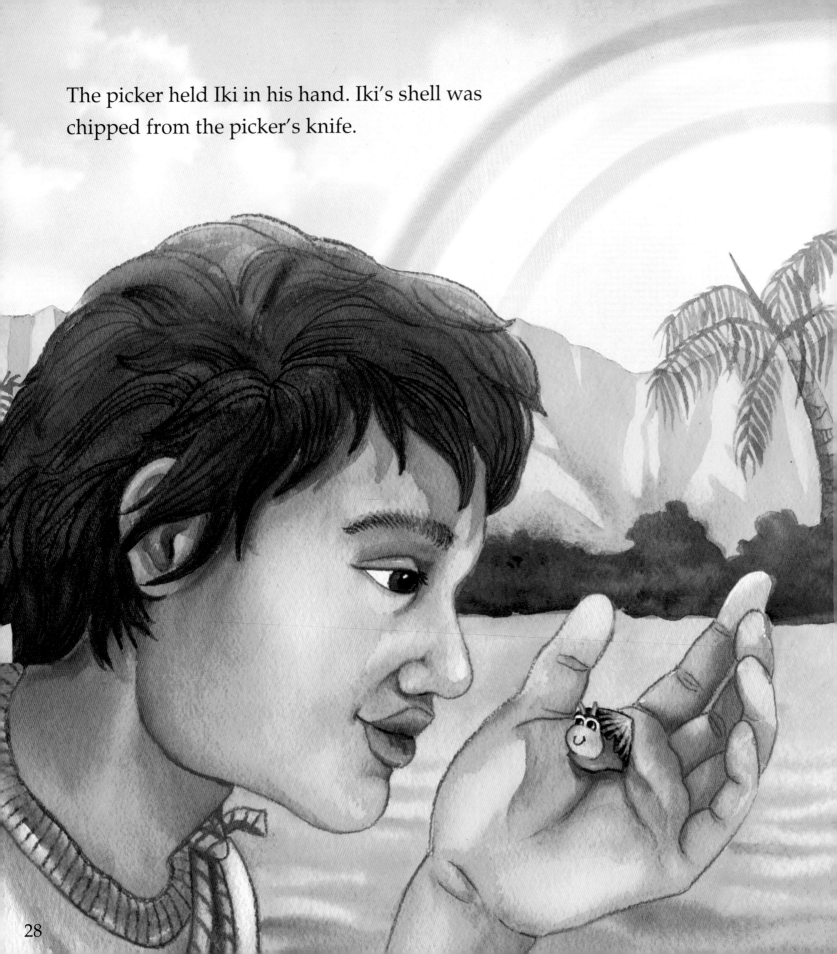

But instead of putting Iki in his bag, the picker placed the little *'opihi* on a rock. Then he opened his bag and released all of Iki's friends.

"You saved my life," said the picker. "You must be my guardian, my *'aumakua*."

From that day on, Iki was loved by all the seashells and was quite famous. Every larva in the ocean knew the story of Iki, the sticky little *'opihi* with the chipped shell.

Iki stuck to it. And what a ride it was!

Can you find Iki's friends?

1. *Kio po'apo'ai* (KEE-o po AH-po aye)
Featherduster worm

2. *Pūpū kōlea* (POO-POO ko-LAY-ah)
Periwinkle snail

3. *'A'ama* (ah AH-mah) Rock crab

4. *Hā'uke'uke* (HA oo-kay oo-kay)
Helmet urchin

5. *Kihikihi* (KEE-hee-KEE-hee)
Moorish idol

6. *Lau wiliwili* (LOW vee-lee-vee-lee)
Milletseed butterflyfish

7. *Hā'uke'uke 'ula'ula*
(HA oo-kay oo-kay oo-lah oo-lah)
Red pencil urchin

8. *Lauhau* (LOW (rhymes with "cow") how)
Fourspot butterflyfish

9. *Pe'a* (PAY-ah) Brittlestar

10. *Leho kiko* (LAY-ho KEE-ko)
Tiger cowry

11. *Pipipi* (pee-PEE-pee)
Black nerite snail

12. *Kīkākapu* (KEE-kah-KAH-poo)
Raccoon butterflyfish

Glossary

'Aumakua **(ow-mah-KU-ah)**
Hawaiian personal or family guardian.

He'e **(HAY ay)**
Octopus.

Larva
The young or immature form of an animal.

'Opihi **(o-PEE-hee)**
A limpet found on Hawai'i's rugged coastline. The larva, or young *opihi*, spend several days drifting with plankton in the ocean before settling onto rocks and developing into limpets. *'Opihi* are delicacies at every Hawaiian luau. Those who pick *'opihi* must be cautious when braving the pounding surf.

Pipipi **(pee-PEE- pee)**
Black nerite snails common on rocks and under ledges at the seashore.

Pūpū kōlea **(POO-POO ko-LAY-ah)**
Speckled gray periwinkle snails found in large colonies above the high tide's reach.